RAINING CATS AND DOGS

I wish, I wish
With all my heart
To fly with dragons
In a land apart.

D1472051

By Irene Trimble
Illustrated by Don Williams
Based on the characters by Ron Rodecker

Visit Dragon Tales on the Web at www.dragontales.com
Watch us on PBS!

One morning, Ord was sorting his dragonball cards when he heard his mother call out, "Ord, did you finish your chores?" Ord had forgotten! He had to fly out the trash . . .

. . . and that it was his turn to fly the dog.

"And it's time you cleaned your room," his mother reminded him. "Don't forget to dust your ceiling before you go out to play."

"Sometimes I wish I couldn't fly at all," Ord said the next day at school. "Then I wouldn't have to spend so much time doing chores."
"That would leave more time for dragonball!" Wheezie agreed.

"Remember—there is a dragonball game today," said their teacher, Quetzal. "But the weather dragon says it's going to rain cats and dogs. Your assignment, *niños,* is to clean up the field after the storm.

"*And,*" Quetzal added, "since Ord feels he is tired of flying today, why not try doing your assignment *without* using your wings?"

Ord and the other dragons hurried out to the playground.
They looked up to see dark clouds gathering.

"We've got to get to the dragonball field fast!" exclaimed Ord. "But it's so far away. How can we get there fast if we can't fly?"

"We may need some help with this no-wing thing," declared Wheezie. "Let's call Max and Emmy. *They* seem to be able to do everything without wings!"

When Max and Emmy appeared in Dragon Land, the dragons told them about the weather dragon's prediction. "That's okay," said Emmy. "When it rains cats and dogs, we just use an umbrella!"

Ord took an umbrella out of his pouch and held it over his head. "Gee, I don't see how this is going to help."

"Oh, so what if you get wet!" exclaimed Max.

"Wet?" asked Ord, puzzled.

Then Cassie interrupted to explain that the dragons weren't supposed to fly. "But we need to get to the dragonball field fast," she added.

Emmy reminded the dragons of a way to get there that was quicker—and lots more fun—than walking. "Let's skip!" she said.

"Good idea! We'll be there in a hop, skip, and a jump that way!"
Wheezie said as they headed for the dragonball field near the
Balloon Tree Forest.

When they reached the field, Max and Emmy got the surprise
of their lives.

The field was covered from end to end with furry little cats and dogs!
"What happened?" Max cried, cuddling a puppy.
"When it rains cats and dogs in this part of Dragon Land, it really *does* rain cats and dogs!" Emmy said with a giggle.

"Now we have to get them back home," said Ord. "*Without* flying."
"And they live way up there!" said Cassie, pointing to the fluffy cloud hovering high above the dragonball field.

"Maybe we can stand on each other's shoulders so whoever's on top can reach the cloud," Wheezie suggested. But they all agreed they might fall.

"We could use a tall ladder," Zak suggested next. They tried, but the puppies and kittens kept climbing back down.

Then Cassie held up a basket. "When I heard it was raining cats and dogs, I put this all in my pouch. Maybe it can help somehow."

"That's it!" shouted Emmy. "Do any of you have some string in your pouches? We can use balloons from the balloon trees to carry the cats and dogs to their cloud!"

Max and Emmy helped their friends pick a bunch of balloons to tie to the basket with bits of yarn, ribbon, and string. While Ord inflated the balloons even more with his hot dragon breath, Cassie coaxed the little dogs and cats into the basket.

Someone needed to help the cats and dogs once they reached the cloud, so Max and Emmy, who were the smallest, climbed in. The others watched as the balloon basket rose up, up, up. In no time, the cats and dogs were back home on their fluffy cloud.

From down below, the dragons noticed that Max and Emmy were having a lot of fun with the cuddly little cats and dogs.

"I bet you can see the whole field from there!" yelled Ord.

"We sure can! Could we stay up here awhile and watch the game?" asked Max, petting the puppy in his lap.

"Okey-dokey, artichokey!" shrieked Wheezie. "See you later!"

"Just let the air out of the balloons really slowly when you come down," Zak added.

So, with puppies, kittens, cats, and dogs nestled all around them, Max and Emmy watched the home runs and fly balls hit by their friends far below.

When it was time for the dragons to return to school, Quetzal watched them skip back. He listened as they told him about their busy no-wing day.

"I am very proud of you, *niños,*" said Quetzal. "You dreamed up a wonderful solution to your problem! Now use your wings to have some fun!"

"Whee!" Max and Emmy hollered, soaring high in the sky.

"Like I always say, it's great to have wings!" Ord said with a smile.